W9-COE-112

Blood in the water
(Scrapbook of America

Scrapbooks of America™

Published by Tradition Books® and distributed to the school and library market by The Child's World®
P.O. Box 326, Chanhassen, MN 55317-0326 ➤ 800/599-READ ➤ http://www.childsworld.com

Photo Credits: Cover: Museum of the City of New York/Corbis; Paul Almasy/Corbis: 17; Bettmann/
Corbis: 13, 15, 21, 24, 31, 34, 35; Horace Bristol/Corbis: 16; Corbis: 9, 12, 25, 37, 40; Richard
Cummins/Corbis: 11; E.O.Hoppe/Corbis: 22 (left); Danny Lehman/Corbis: 22 (right); Stephanie Maze/
Corbis: 7; David Muench/Corbis: 10, 39; Museum of the City of New York/Corbis: 28; Royalty-Free/
Corbis: 6, 30; Nik Wheeler/Corbis: 18

An Editorial Directions book
Editorial Directions, Inc.: E. Russell Primm, Editorial Director; Lucia Raatma, Line Editor, Photo Selec-
tor, and Additional Writing; Katie Marsico, Assistant Editor; Olivia Nellums, Editorial Assistant; Susan
Hindman, Copy Editor; Susan Ashley, Proofreader; Alice Flanagan, Photo Researcher and Additional Writer

Design: The Design Lab

Library of Congress Cataloging-in-Publication Data
Cataloging-in-Publication data for this title has been applied for and is available from the United States
Library of Congress.

Scrapbooks of America™

Blood in the Water
A Story of Friendship during the Mexican War

by Pamela Dell

TRADITION BOOKS®
A New Tradition in Children's Publishing™

MAPLE PLAIN, MINNESOTA

One early spring morning in the year 1846, my grandmother, Doña Clarita, raised her palm above a bowl of clear water, her fingers outstretched like long, bony, brown twigs. Her eyes closed and she began to mumble soft words to herself. Then her fingers started to move as if they were playing on piano keys, or perhaps feeling for tiny invisible **currents** flowing between her hand and the water's surface.

As I watched, the water began to cloud and swirl, and a mist seemed to rise up from the bowl, until I could no longer make out its blue-colored rim. At last, Doña Clarita opened her eyes. Her gaze was focused far away, as if she were looking at something only

When most people look into a bowl of water, they see only a reflection. But my grandmother could look at the water and see the future.

Like Doña Clarita, many curanderos use potions and tonics to heal other people.

visible to her. She bent forward and peered into the mist rising from the bowl.

"*Sangre*," she said, and I heard pain in her voice. "*Mucho sangre*, much blood. Much more blood to come."

"*Abuela*. Grandmother," I whispered, "teach me to see as you do."

After a moment, her deep, dark eyes met mine. "Some things, *niña*, you do not want to see," she replied.

Though our family now lived on land just outside the town of Corpus Christi, in the **territory** called Texas, my grandmother had come from the south of Mexico, from Vera Cruz. There, in that place and in the surrounding jungles, lived many *curanderos*— ones with powers to heal or to harm. Ones who knew the secrets of herbs and spells and lucky charms to ward off evil.

Doña Clarita never claimed to be a curandera. What powers she had, she kept mostly private. But I knew she had seen, and had perhaps even learned, much of such things during her long life in Vera Cruz. I knew she held mysteries in her mind, even if she did not reveal them. But sometimes she would look into the mist of the blue bowl, and when she did, she usually saw correctly what was to come.

Sangre. Blood. I did not need any powers of my own to understand what she was talking about. I knew that only the year before, *Los Estados Unidos*, the United States, had claimed Texas as its own.

The word they had used was **annexed** and it meant that, to Americans, Texas had already been accepted as another state in their ever-growing Union. But we Mexicans still believed the land of Texas to be rightfully ours.

True, we had many fewer people than the States and not many of us had ventured so far north. Not many, as Papá proudly put it, were as adventurous as our own family, who had come to this **fertile** land at the mouth of the Nueces River even before I had been born. Also, three-quarters of the blood that flowed in Papá's veins was Spanish, so for him it had been easier to acquire land than it was for many others.

It was also true that our leaders in

The Nueces River is 338 miles (545 kilometers) long.

Vera Cruz was the first Spanish settlement in Mexico. It was founded by explorer Hernando Cortés in the 1500s.

My grandmother spent much of her life in Vera Cruz, a beautiful port city in Mexico.

Mexico City had agreed to allow Americans to settle in the **vast** emptiness of that Texas territory. But they had intended that settlement to extend only as far as the Nueces River and no farther west than that. Now these northerners, with their booming population and their unending appetite for exploration and new settlements, had pushed well past the Nueces. They had rolled onward right to the very banks of the mighty Rio Grande, and they were boldly calling the miles and miles of land between the two rivers theirs as well.

To our people this was outrage. The land of Texas belonged to Mexico and had been ours ever since we had won our **independence**

The Rio Grande is one of the longest rivers in North America, flowing for 1,885 miles (3,034 km).

The Rio Grande is a sight to see. That river proved to be an important boundary in the war between the United States and Mexico.

Sitting in our warm kitchen, my brothers and I listened to the stories Doña Clarita and Papá would tell.

from Spain years earlier. So who had now given it to the Americans? Was it theirs just for the taking? I did not have answers to these questions, but it was no wonder to me that Doña Clarita saw days of blood to come.

To bargain would be weak, my Papá assured us. The offer of money was an insult. We would not let our leaders sell us out to the Americans, even though, according to him, they had been trying to make deals at every turn. And were we Mexicans just going to sit back and allow the **invaders** to roll over us, Papá wanted to know. "No!" he had boomed, after posing the question to the family as we sat at our supper one night. "We will fight against them as long as we have the might! My sons will fight the dogs of the North, the

11

Yanquis, for the land that has long belonged to us!"

Papá had looked to my brothers, all four of them in turn, and each had nodded in agreement. My two elder sisters and I, as well as Mamá and Grandmother, too, had said nothing. But with whatever small powers of mind-reading I possessed, I felt certain that they were all as terrified as I was. None of us could bear the thought of my father's sons going off to war against America. I had bowed my head then and asked the Heavenly Father to bless and protect all of us, to keep us far from danger.

But in those early days of 1846, even before Doña Clarita saw blood in the water, danger—and the very real threat of war—did

12

The city of Austin in the1840s, soon after becoming the capital of Texas

In 1810, the people of Mexico rose up against the Spanish who ruled them. The war lasted for eleven years, and 600,000 lives were lost. But in 1821, Mexico declared its independence from Spain.

As a soldier, General Zachary Taylor earned the nickname "Old Rough and Ready."

General Zachary Taylor, the leader of the U.S. troops who had been stationed in Corpus Christi for months.

seem to lurk all around us. Papá and my brothers spoke constantly of our country's troubles, so that even I, a girl of twelve, knew many of the details. I knew, for example, that nearly 4,000 American troops had been stationed in Corpus Christi since the summer before. I had seen their **encampment** stretching forever along the banks of the bay, row after row of scraggly tents. I had seen how they had built up the embankments with sand and pieces of twisted **mesquite** wood to ward off the damp winter winds. I had been chilled by the sight of their huge horses and their guns and the fierce, determined eyes of the soldiers. Once I had even seen their commander, General Zachary Taylor, on his horse, which people said he called Old Whitey.

13

And then, in March, only a few weeks before my grandmother looked into her Seeing Bowl, the American troops were gone. They had moved south, in the direction of the Rio Grande, perhaps to spill blood there. But the talk of war remained in the minds and in the mouths of everyone left in our town, adults and children alike.

Even my friend Carmen, who cared little about such things, now spoke of it.

"My father says there will be war for sure if the Mexicans refuse to recognize the Americans' possession of Texas all the way to the Rio Grande," Carmen said to me as we walked toward her house from the waterfront. It was the second week of May and I had come into town with Papá, as I usually did when the business of running our ranch took him into Corpus Christi.

While Papá made deals for the sale of horses or cattle at the trading post on the **bluff,** I would call for Carmen at her home in town and we would go walking. Our footsteps often took us along the strand, the strip of land that ran between the bay and the bluff, and then on to the waterfront. As we walked there, we watched the sailors from shipping vessels passing in and out of the few buildings scattered along the water's edge. To amuse ourselves, we would make a game of it, trying to guess what country each man had come from, or where he was off to, and what goods his ship carried. If we tired of that, we might go to dig in the plentiful oyster beds

A ceremony for Texas's official statehood. It wouldn't be long before my home was considered part of Texas instead of Mexico.

for delicious treasures to take home. In warm weather, after we returned to Carmen's house, we sometimes sat in the small courtyard with something cool to drink until it was time for me to leave.

That particular day the air was heavy with a welcome warmth, and the sun on my back felt good. But my heart was carrying a burden, and my steps were heavy. As Carmen and I walked, I noticed as always the glances thrown our way. When the two of us strolled together, passers-by often looked at us with curiosity, or with coldness, and sometimes even with undisguised hostility. I knew it was because we had differences that, in the eyes of too many people, should have prevented us from being friends.

I loved spending time with Carmen, usually in a shady spot in her home's courtyard.

Children of pure Spanish blood were considered to be in a higher social class than I was.

Carmen's family was of pure Spanish stock, having come from Florida to settle in the Texas territory only a year earlier, after Florida had become an American state. They were proud, I knew, of both their pure bloodline and of now being citizens of the United States, a country they saw as powerful and bold. But I was a *mestiza,* with a mixture of both Indian and Spanish blood running in my veins. So although Carmen and I had the Spanish language in common, Carmen's social class was considered higher than my own, by both blood and citizenship. But we had stumbled on a secret truth: Between true friends these differences were nothing but a useless detail. And that is how we treated them, even if others were so easily offended.

The gates of Chapultepec Castle in Mexico. In the months to come, U.S. troops would overtake that castle and everything would change.

But now, with Mexico and America both pawing the ground and preparing to butt heads like two *toros*—two furious bulls— competing for the same pasture, I worried that Carmen and I would end up with a fence between us.

"Why should we recognize America's claim?" I challenged. "This is our land, not theirs."

Carmen's eyes rested on me, and for once I could not tell what she was thinking. "My father would not agree," she said quietly. I did not want to argue, and I felt confusion burning on the inside of my head.

We walked on in silence and then, as we neared Carmen's house, my mouth opened and I found myself telling her what Doña Clarita had seen in the water. I could not help but voice my fears for my brothers at the end, too.

"Even Luís and Pedro have gone south to Matamoros in hopes of joining the troops of General Arista there!" I told her. "They left last month, and we've barely heard a word of them yet."

"And what of your two younger brothers?" Carmen replied.

"Fernando and Tomás? They are barely older than I am, so for now they are still at home. But if things get worse, I am afraid Papá will be encouraging them to join the cause, too."

"I cannot believe we will have a war," Carmen said. "If only Mexico would just accept the offers put out by our government, none of this would happen! And your current president should simply honor the fact that Santa Anna before him gave all of Texas to the United States."

"What?" We were nearly right in front of Carmen's house now but her words stopped me in my tracks. I felt a shiver go down my spine, as if the first stakes in the fence had been driven into the ground between us. "Carmen, Santa Anna is in **exile**—and crazy, according to Papá, for trying to weave deals against his own people!"

Carmen did not answer so I continued, but I wondered if I was trying to convince her or myself. "But no matter what he agreed to," I said, "I am sure it was not that

America should have all the land between this river and the Rio Grande."

Carmen's delicate black eyebrows rose as she looked at me. "Don't be so sure, Bonita," she said, as if she knew more than I did somehow. Then she took my hand and squeezed it, and pulled me along with her up to the front door. "But anyway, let's not talk of these problems any longer. I'm so tired of it! And I didn't tell you—my cousin's here to visit! All the way from San Antonio."

I had heard from Carmen all about the glories of her cousin Rafael. But instead of feeling eager to finally meet him, my mind was caught in a swirl of entirely differ-ent thoughts: Carmen's troubling words. Thoughts of my brothers aiming guns at other

General Santa Anna and two of his men. Though he was in exile before the war, he returned to fight against the United States.

Santa Anna was president of Mexico before the war, but he was removed from office. During the war, he returned and fought for Mexico. He later became president of the country again.

My adobe home was a peaceful
and precious place for me.

Mesquite trees grew in the fields near my home.

men and being aimed at in return. Wondering how it all would end.

"Where's Rafael?" Carmen asked, as we came together into the front hall. Her mother greeted me coolly, with a quick nod. If she did not entirely approve of her daughter's friendship with me, she had never said a word of it to me, and she had not prevented it.

"He will return shortly," her mother replied. "But Bonita should be going now. We have some things to do around the house, daughter. She can meet him next time."

❦

As Papá and I turned the bend in the road, I could see our house glowing like a pearl in the rays of the setting sun and, as always, I admired it. Like many dwellings in our town, it was made of **shellcrete,** a mixture of crushed oyster shells and clay, which was then hardened in the sun to make a solid, smooth **adobe.** The house always seemed to glisten as we approached from the distance, and gazing upon that familiar scene—the house, the grazing lands, the windswept mesquite trees, the rose and amber streaks in the western sky—always gave me a feeling of deep peace. It was a scene so peaceful that it seemed impossible to me that war or its effects might ever touch us. But on this day my peace did not last long.

As our wagon pulled up to the house, Mamá came rushing out, frantic. In the next moment, **chaos** broke out all around us as my brothers and sisters streamed outside behind her. I saw Doña Clarita looking solemn as she stood in the doorway.

"It has begun!" Mamá cried, even before Papá had his two feet on the ground. "We have heard from Uncle Silva! There have been two days of fighting on the plains to the south! He sends word that Pedro has been injured, and Luís is missing!" With this last bit of news, Mama's voice crumpled, and the voices of my brothers and sisters rose all at once in excited chatter, trying to fill us in on what they had learned.

It seemed that at the end of April, the Mexican troops waiting in Matamoros had finally **ventured** north across the Rio Grande. There, they had surprised and successfully fought a group of American troops at Rancho

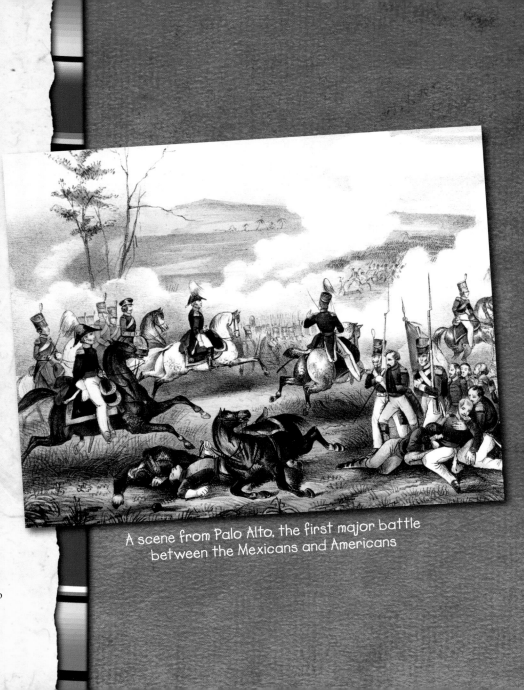

A scene from Palo Alto, the first major battle between the Mexicans and Americans

As Doña Clarita predicted, much blood was spilled on both sides during the war.

de Carricitos. A few days later, the Mexican soldiers had surrounded Fort Texas, coming from all directions. Then, on May 8, the first major clash had taken place, with fierce hand-to-hand combat on the wide Palo Alto prairie. The Americans had come out the victors in that fight, despite there being many more Mexican troops.

The following morning, the Yanquis pursued our troops to the banks of Resaca de la Palma. After another bloody battle there throughout the afternoon, the U.S. soldiers had again won out and had chased our men back over the Rio Grande. There had been losses on both sides, Uncle Silva reported. But our Mexican troops had suffered far worse, with many more deaths and injuries,

25

including Pedro's, and the unknown fate of Luís. He feared that we had lost the lower Rio Grande valley.

"But what has happened to my brothers?" I broke in. "And what will happen to us?!"

"We will fight on!" Papá exclaimed. "This is a war of honor! We shall never admit American independence in Texas until we are dead." Looking at him and the dark flame in his eyes, I feared it would come to that. America would liberate us from what it believed was our **unstable** and **impoverished** government and give us peace through conquest, oh yes. But what would it cost in the lives of our people?

❦

Three days later, Pedro returned home in my uncle's wagon. His head was bandaged. He had a deep gash in his upper arm, and his clothes were in shreds. But the worst part was that he could not speak, and the doctors did not know if his condition would be permanent. We still had heard no word of Luís.

The next afternoon, when I went with Papá into town, the streets were full of more people than I had ever seen before. On every corner we passed, men stood and talked. Many more shouted and shook newspapers in each others' faces. Hearing the rising and falling voices, speaking in both Spanish and English, I wished only that I could turn it all off and let none of it into my own ears. These men wanted war. They were excited by the idea of such a venture, by the heat of battle. I could not understand it.

All I could understand was that I had one wounded brother, another one missing, or fighting somewhere I knew not where, and two more brothers determined to go off and join the **conflict** themselves. If any sound had made sense to me in that moment, it would have been only the sound of my own voice screaming against this terrible, senseless **fury** all around me.

So it was that the soft peacefulness inside Carmen's home that afternoon was a great relief to me. Carmen came skipping down the long hall toward me with a smile on her face and, for the moment, the outside world faded away. I was with my friend, and things were good again.

"Bonita!" she said. "I'm so glad you're here. You must come with Rafael and me to Mann's red house!"

Carmen's words startled me. She was speaking of the new hotel, Mann's Virginia House, at the corner of Water Street and Cooper's Alley. It had been built the year before and, at three stories high, it was the tallest and grandest building in town. I wanted nothing more than to glimpse the inside of that place. But I was not certain I would be welcome there.

When I did not reply, Carmen laughed. "Don't worry," she said. "If we are with Rafael, it will be safe. He is seventeen already. We'll just sit in the lovely courtyard and watch the people for a while and then return home." She turned her face toward the hallway and shouted.

BATTLE OF RESACA DE LA PALMA MAY 9TH 1846.

Capture of Genl. VEGA by the gallant Capt. MAY.

The Battle of Resaca de la Palma was another loss for our Mexican troops.

"Rafael! Come quickly! Let us go now!"

There was the sound of heavy footsteps on the tiles, and I turned to see Rafael coming toward us. At once I recognized the haughty beauty I had seen in the faces of other young men of pure Spanish blood, and I understood why Carmen made such a fuss over him. He had fine, sharply cut features, graceful hands, and eyes that shone with a hard, intelligent brilliance.

Rafael held out his hand when Carmen introduced me, but he did not smile. *They are Americans,* I thought and then immediately tried to push the thought from my mind.

❦

At Mann's red house, Rafael arranged for

drinks for us and sweets to eat, and we settled in a shady part of the courtyard. With the approach of each unfamiliar person, I waited nervously to be asked to leave. But no one said such words, and I began to relax a little, deciding that being with Carmen and Rafael shielded me from such humiliation.

As Carmen chattered on about a new dress that was being made for her, I stole a glance at Rafael. His handsome face was a mask of boredom. But I was tongue-tied in his presence and could not think of a single new line of conversation. I put my head down and studied my own far less fancy **smock**, suddenly embarrassed.

Finally, Rafael put an end to Carmen's

talking. "So!" he said brightly. I looked up and found his eyes on me, and perhaps laughing at me—I couldn't be sure. "Señorita Bonita! Tell me, what do you think of this war we have entered into now?"

"But we haven't yet, have we?" I said, unsure. "Not officially, I mean?" Rafael laughed, and Carmen looked uncomfortable.

"Do you not read?" he said. "Of course we have! I have just read it myself today in the paper. On May 13, President Polk declared war on Mexico. Wait, let me remember!"

Rafael paused with a finger to his temple and a slight smile, a harsh smile, on his face.

"Oh, Rafael!" Carmen burst out. "Must we talk of this here and now?!"

We shared a cool drink at Mann's red house, but our conversation was unsettling for me.

Before becoming president of the United States, James K. Polk served in the House of Representatives and as governor of Tennessee.

James K. Polk was president of the United States during the war with Mexico.

"Ah, we must, little cousin," said Rafael. "As it stated in the paper, 'the Mexicans have invaded our territory and shed the blood of our fellow citizens on our own soil' and that is—"

"But it is *not* your own soil!" I protested, standing and facing him. "Why do you Americans think you can just come in and call it all yours? It's unbelievable!"

Carmen took hold of my wrist and gently pulled me back to sit beside her, but my face flamed still with anger. She kept her hand firmly around my arm and I allowed it, as if her touch might restore my peace.

But Rafael's look of superiority sickened me. "Believe me," he said calmly, "our

conquering Mexico is a blessing for you people, you'll see."

"'You people'!" I said scornfully. "And how can you call invasion a blessing?!"

"Firstly, we have not invaded. The Rio Grande is the western border of our newest state," he replied. "And now think! Your country is continually in political upheaval. Every week someone new is calling himself president. Not only that, your government is deeply in debt to the United States, too. At least maybe now those debts will be forgiven. We will show you how peace and **democracy** work."

It was clear to me that Rafael knew much more than I did about this clash between our two countries, and I had few words with which to fight back.

"*Puercos!*" I said, but softly. "Pigs!"

Rafael put back his head and laughed heartily, as if I had made a good joke. But I was sure I felt more anger toward him in that moment than I had ever felt for anyone in my life. It was seeping out toward Carmen now, too. As if she sensed it, her fingers tightened around my wrist, and she looked from me to Rafael.

"Many Americans agree with Bonita, Rafael," she said to him quietly. "They think this expansion is wrong of us. Many important people are speaking out against it."

"Wrong?" Rafael's eyebrow arched and he looked down his long, fine nose at her. I saw plainly the hard humor in his eyes.

"Yes!" she said stubbornly. "For one thing,

they say it's just to gain more slave territory. Many Americans think we have enough territory as it is, so why take more?"

"Important people!" Rafael scoffed. "These are people who have no understanding at all of Manifest Destiny."

There was a pause in which none of us spoke. A yellow dog **lumbered** past, and Rafael threw him some tidbits and then flicked his hand to **shoo** the animal away. I did not want to have to be the one to ask, but it seemed that Carmen might already know these words. Was I to just sit there not knowing what he meant?

"What's that?" I said finally, but I could hear the unhappiness in my own voice.

"Manifest Destiny," Rafael repeated slowly, as if I had little ability to understand spoken language. "I am referring to America's **divinely** appointed mission to lead the world to a higher, more perfect civilization. We will move west until we have taken not only Texas, but New Mexico, California, all of it to the Pacific Ocean. That is clearly the destiny of this nation. To bring light to the darkness that still swallows the western portion of this continent. And, in fact, much of the world. "

My breath came short and shallow, and I jerked my arm from Carmen's grasp as I stood up again.

"Not everyone believes that!" I exclaimed. "It's impossible!"

"Bonita—" Carmen said, trying to settle things.

"I must go." I was afraid by now that the scene we were creating might bring more attention in the courtyard than it already had. Above everything else, I feared being asked to leave. Was I standing now on foreign soil? Rafael answered that for me as I hurried toward the street, ignoring Carmen's calls to me.

"Bonita!" he cried out behind me. "Be happy! You are an American now! Like us!" His laughter was so full of humor that I picked up my step and ran, unable to stand the sound of it.

The blood that my grandmother saw in her Seeing Bowl was indeed much. And it ran for a long time. The Americans pushed ever

Not all Americans were in favor of the war with Mexico. In fact, former president John Quincy Adams was even against the annexation of Texas.

At the Battle of Buena Vista, the Mexican troops far outnumbered the U.S. soldiers. But the Americans claimed victory again.

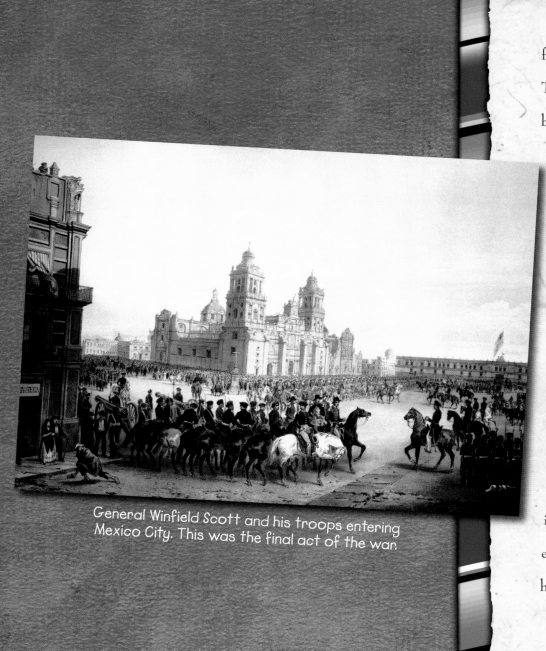

General Winfield Scott and his troops entering Mexico City. This was the final act of the war.

farther south over the next year and a half. They conquered us in one town after another, bringing much humiliation, disease, and despair to our people. Finally they raised their flag over the National Palace in our capital, Mexico City, and everyone knew we were lost.

"The Americans may have been our enemy in this battle, yes," Doña Clarita said to me when we heard this news. "But remember, niña, the much greater enemy is the desire for war itself. That is what cripples and destroys us. Men will always have differences of opinion. But it is the way in which they go about settling those differences that determines if we will be free of the horrors and grief of war."

In the last of it, at Chapultepec Castle, young Mexican men jumped to their deaths rather than be captured by U.S. troops. If Doña Clarita had glimpsed beforehand in her bowl what was to happen to them, or to my brothers, she did not let on. Pedro mended, but his mind was slower, and he rarely spoke at all anymore. Eventually Luís's body was found washed up on the banks of the Rio Grande. They said he had drowned while trying to swim the river during the retreat from Resaca de la Palma. Even before Luís's body was recovered, Fernando and Tomás went off together to fight at Monterrey. In battle there, Fernando was killed by gunfire. Because of unsanitary conditions in the camps, Tomás contracted a dread disease, abandoned the fight, and came home. He died a week later, as I sat at his bedside holding tight to his hand and trying to keep back my tears.

Finally, on February 2, 1848, the war was brought to an end with the signing of the Treaty of Guadalupe-Hidalgo. The **treaty** took away nearly half the land that had once belonged to our country, and it divided Mexico from the United States along the Rio Grande. That meant that our family was now living on U.S. soil. We didn't know for sure anymore where we belonged, whether we were Mexican or American, nor who would claim us. But Doña Clarita saw rightly

The phrase "Manifest Destiny" was first used in 1845 by John L. O'Sullivan in an article he wrote about the annexation of Texas.

The treaty of Guadulpe-Hidalgo was signed in February 1848, and the fighting finally ended.

The United States gained more than 525,000 square miles (1,360,000 square kilometers) of territory as a result of the Mexican War.

that our long-held family lands would be taken from us by the Yanquis, though it took some years for that to occur.

In the summer of 1848, I asked my grandmother to look again into her Seeing Bowl. I wanted her to peer into the mist and tell me what she saw for my friendship with Carmen. Carmen and I had seen each other only a few more times after the visit to the hotel with Rafael. As the war progressed, we had gradually grown apart, despite our desire to keep that from happening. We had indeed become fenced off from each other because of our differing beliefs, just as I had feared. Now that some measure of peace had been restored, I missed my friendship with her, our conversations, and our long walks along the waterfront.

"Look and tell me what you see, Grandmother," I begged, sitting beside her.

"It is not in the bowl that you will find this answer, niña," she responded, placing her hand, old but still strong, on mine. "You must look into your heart instead, and see what is waiting for you there. At one time you and your friend were not afraid of your differences. They were a delight to you, not a barrier. You had respect and tolerance for one another's outlook on the world, even if you did not feel the same way yourself. Is that not true?"

I nodded, remembering.

"Then do not be afraid to look deep into the bowl of your own heart, granddaughter," Doña Clarita said. "If you find those feelings still there, then you will have success in bringing your friendship back to life."

The next time I went into town with Papá, I asked him to drop me on the street where Carmen lived. This surprised him, I could tell. He still harbored a burning hatred of the Yanquis, but he agreed to my request, allowing me the freedom to decide for myself how I should feel.

My heart was pounding as I drew near Carmen's house. It had been a while. But I was an American now. Or rather, I was someone who now needed to understand more clearly exactly who and what I

After the war, the familiar land around me was still home, but it was no longer Mexico.

truly was. It came to me that maybe my once-dear friend could help me to understand this.

I paused and glanced to the window of Carmen's bedroom and was surprised to see a face framed there between the colorful curtains. It was a familiar face. A face I loved. For a moment that face gazed back at me in a serious, studious way. Then I raised my hand slightly, hopefully, and when I did, she smiled.

I felt certain then that somehow Carmen and I would find our way in these new circumstances. I knew we would manage, even if it took a while, to tear down the fence that had grown up between us. ❦

The History of the U.S.-Mexican War

Twelve-year-old Bonita lived during a stormy time. In the 1840s, different beliefs about the future of Texas were dividing the young territory. Bonita's family lived in Texas, but most of them were born in Mexico. They were *mestizo*, loyal citizens of Indian and Spanish ancestry, and they believed that Texas belonged to Mexico. Carmen's ancestors were from Spain. Her family had moved to Texas from Florida, where relatives had once settled and become U.S. citizens. They, like many Anglo-Americans living in Texas, wanted Texas to become a state in the Union. These families shared a common language and similar traditions, but their loyalties to different countries divided them. In 1846, such strong differences erupted into the Mexican War (1846–1848).

U.S. citizens had begun colonizing Texas after Mexico had won its own war for independence from Spain in 1821. When Mexico stopped emigration of U.S. settlers to Texas in 1830, Texans rebelled. Five years later, the problem had turned into war. Texans quickly defeated Mexican forces and established the Republic of Texas in April 1836. Mexico, however, never accepted the loss of Texas and for the next ten years considered it to be Mexican territory under the temporary rule of a rebel government.

When the Republic of Texas became a U.S. state on December 29, 1845, Mexican leaders threatened to invade Texas to reclaim the lost province. U.S. troops went into Texas to thwart the invasion. After being attacked by Mexican troops on April 24, 1846, the United States declared war. During the war, which lasted nearly a year and half, American forces overwhelmed the Mexican troops fighting battles in Texas, New Mexico, California, and Mexico. On September 13, 1847, the U.S. Army under General Winfield Scott occupied Mexico City, which brought the war to an end.

On February 2, 1848, both sides signed the Treaty of Guadalupe Hidalgo. The treaty, which is still in force today, set the Rio Grande as the southern border of Texas. It required Mexico hand over to the United States all the territory that today includes the states of California, Arizona, New Mexico, Nevada, Utah, and parts of Colorado and Wyoming. In return for land, the United States gave Mexico $15 million and paid off some of its debts.

Glossary

adobe a kind of brick made of clay mixed with straw and dried in the sun

annexed taken or controlled by force

bluff a high, steep bank

chaos loud confusion

conflict a serious disagreement or war

conquering defeating and taking over

currents the movements of air or water, usually in a river or ocean

democracy a type of government in which leaders are elected by the people

divinely related to the actions or wishes of God

encampment a place where people set up camp

exile sent away from one's country and told not to return

fertile good for growing crops and other plants

fury violent anger

impoverished poor; without basic food or housing

Timeline

1821 Mexico gains its independence from Spain.

1835 Texas revolts against the Mexican government, which controls the region.

1836 Texans establish the Republic of Texas, but Mexico refuses to recognize the territory's independence.

1844 James K. Polk is elected president of the United States.

1845 In March, Congress votes to annex Texas. In the fall, President Polk sends John Slidell to talk to the Mexican officials. He is to offer them $25 million if they agree to the Rio Grande boundary and sell New Mexico and California to the United States. The government officials refuse to see him. On December 29, Texas becomes the twenty-eighth state in the Union. Mexico reacts by breaking off all talks with the United States.

independence freedom from the control of others

invaders people who enter a country or region and take it over

lumbered moved along clumsily

mesquite certain spiny trees and shrubs common in the American Southwest

shellcrete a building material made of crushed oyster shells and clay

shoo to send away

smock a long, loose shirt sometimes worn over other clothing

territory a large area of land; region

treaty a formal agreement between two groups of people

unstable not steady; always changing

vast wide, open space

ventured did something risky or dangerous

1846 In April, General Zachary Taylor leads U.S. troops to the Nueces River; the battles of Palo Alto and Resaca de la Palma take place on May 8 and 9; on May 13, the U.S. Congress declares war on Mexico.

1847 In March, General Winfield Scott leads U.S. troops in the capture of Vera Cruz; in April they take the Mexican capital.

1848 A peace treaty is signed at the village of Guadalupe-Hidalgo.

Activities

Continuing the Story

(Writing Creatively)

Continue Bonita's story. Elaborate on an event from her scrapbook or add your own entries to the beginning or end of her journal. You might write about Bonita's experiences during the war or how her life changed once the war was over. You can also write your own short story of historical fiction about the U.S.-Mexican War and how it affected family life in both countries.

Celebrating Your Heritage

(Discovering Family History)

Research your own family history. Find out if any of your relatives were involved directly or indirectly in the war with Mexico. Were your relatives Mexican, Mexican-American, or American? Which side did they support? Ask family members to write down what they know about the people and events of this era.

Documenting History

(Exploring Community History)

Find out how your city or town was affected by the war. Visit your library, a historical society, a museum, or related Web sites for links to important people and events. What did newspapers report at the time? When, where, why, and how did your community respond? Who was involved? What was the outcome?

Preserving Memories

(Crafting)

Make a scrapbook about family life in Texas during the mid-1800s or about a soldier's life during the U.S.-Mexican War. Imagine what life was like for them. Fill the pages with special events, stories, interviews, songs, and drawings of memorabilia. Include copies of newspaper clippings, postcards, posters, diaries, citizenship papers, and other historical records. Decorate the pages and cover of your scrapbook with pictures of family heirlooms, household items, army equipment, maps, and traditional Mexican objects.

To Find Out More

At the Library

Carey, Charles W. Jr. *The Mexican War: Mr. Polk's War.*
Berkeley Heights, N.J.: Enslow, 2002.

Carter, Alden R. *The Mexican War: Manifest Destiny.*
Danbury, Conn.: Franklin Watts, 1999.

Collier, Christopher, and James Lincoln Collier. *Hispanic America, Texas, and the Mexican War, 1835–1850.* Tarrytown, N.Y.: Benchmark, 1998.

Jacobs, William Jay. *War with Mexico.* Brookfield, Conn.: Millbrook Press, 1993.

Tibbitts, Alison Davis. *James K. Polk.* Berkeley Heights, N.J.: Enslow, 1999.

On the Internet

Descendants of Mexican War Veterans
http://www.dmwv.org/mexwar/concise.htm
For more history of the war

The Mexican-American War Memorial Homepage
http://sunsite.unam.mx/revistas/1847
To learn about the war and its long-term effects

U.S.-Mexican War
http://www.pbs.org/kera/usmexicanwar/
A companion site to the PBS documentary about the war

Places to Visit

Mexican Heritage Plaza
1700 Alum Rock Avenue
San Jose, CA 95116
800/642-8482
To see exhibits and attend Mexican cultural events

National Hispanic Cultural Center of New Mexico
1701 4th Street, S.W.
Albuquerque, NM 87102
505/246-2261
To learn more about Hispanic art and history

Palo Alto Battlefield National Historic Site
1623 Central Boulevard
Suite 213
Brownsville, TX 78520
956/541-2785
To visit this famous battlefield, north of downtown
Brownsville; tours begin from the visitors' center

Pío Pico State Historic Park
6003 Pioneer Boulevard
Whittier, CA 90606
562/695-1217
To tour the home of the last Mexican
governor of California

ABOUT THE AUTHOR

Pamela Dell has been making her living as a writer for about fifteen years. Though she has published both fiction and nonfiction for adults, in the last decade she has written mostly for kids. Her nonfiction work includes biographies, science, history, and nature topics. She has also published contemporary and historical fiction, as well as award-winning interactive multimedia. The twelve books in the Scrapbooks of America series have been some of her favorite writing projects.